The

CHILDREN'S
CHRISTMAS CAROL

The CHILDREN'S

Adapted by DARLENE GEIS

Illustrated by DANIEL NOONAN

PRENTICE – HALL • *Incorporated*

CHRISTMAS CAROL

By JOHANNA SPYRI

Author of HEIDI

ENGLEWOOD CLIFFS · NEW JERSEY

CONTENTS

CHAPTER ONE

WINTER IN THE ALPS

HIGH IN the Swiss Alps, where the children lived, winter had come early that year. The little village of Altdorf lay at the foot of a high mountain snuggled cozily under its white eiderdown of snow. But to get to the home of the children whose story this is, we must climb a long hard way above the village.

A narrow path leads out of the village across a snowy meadow and along the Schachen Brook. In summer, this brook is a wild and raging torrent, tumbling and leaping down the mountainside. Many tourists come to visit it, not only because of its wild beauty, but also because there is a legend that this is the spot where William Tell, the great Swiss hero, was drowned.

Now, in winter, the brook is smaller and quieter and nearly frozen over with ice. A crude wooden bridge crosses it close to the mountain, and from there a steep little path leads up the rocky slope. The slope itself is bare of all except a few scattered huts half buried in the snow and perched at tipsy angles on the steep ground.

The smallest of these looks like a toy house with a door so low that a grown-up man could not enter without bending down. Next to it is a stable so small that only a very skinny goat would have room in it. The children's goat is very skinny, indeed, and so fits snugly into her stable.

Now, this tiny hut is the one we have been looking for, the one where Barty, his sister, Franzeli, and their Mother live. It has not been an easy life for them.

When the Father was alive, things were much better. But he has been gone for four years. In the old days, the Father used to go to work each morning and come home at night, bringing a loaf of bread and other food for the family, and gathering enough grass and hay to keep the goat well fed. The mother had worked aound the house, making good cheese from the goat's extra milk and knitting warm clothes for the family. They lived quietly and peacefully, and only left their little house together when they all went down to the village to Church.

The little boy had been born on St. Sebastian's Day, and so he was named after the Saint. But he was called Barty for short. His younger sister was born on the Day of Saint Francis, so they baptised her Francisca, and called her Franzeli.

The two children were the most precious things in their Mother's life. And after she had lost her husband, they were her only joy on earth and her greatest comfort. She kept them so clean and tidy, that no one who saw them would have guessed that they lived in the tiniest house and were the children of one of the poorest women in the whole neighborhood.

Each morning, the boy and girl were carefully washed, and Franzeli's light blond curls were brushed until they shone. Every Sunday morning the Mother dressed the children in a freshly washed shirt—one of the two each child owned. With her shirt, Franzeli wore the better of her two skirts. And Barty wore the trousers that had been made over for him from his Father's. This was all they had and all they needed, for all through the warm and golden summer they wore neither shoes nor socks. In the winter, they had warm clothing that their Mother had knitted for them; it was not much, nor did they need more clothes, for in the bitter Alpine winter they hardly ever left their little house.

With all the work that had to be done, the Mother was busy from dawn till dusk, and had no time for pleasure at all. But she did not mind the hard work as long as she had her two little ones with her. When Barty and Franzeli greeted their Mother with cheerful smiles, she forgot her weariness and thought to herself, "I would not take the most comfortable life in the world in exchange for my children."

Indeed, the children were loved by everyone who saw them. When they went down the slopes together, six-year-old Barty, wanting to protect his little sister, held her small hand firmly in his. The two bright-haired and smiling children seemed to have a special glow about them, and many a neighbor watching them pass, hand in hand, would say, "I have never seen children look so happy and so lovely."

Sometimes, one of the village women would speak to the Mother, "How I admire your children! Barty looks like a rosy apple, and Franzeli, with her delicate face and golden hair, reminds me of the angel in our Church."

But the Mother did not think the children's appearance should matter so much. So she would reply to all compliments, "I only pray that the good Lord may keep them healthy and will let them grow up to be good people." And every day she did pray for just that, faithfully.

CHAPTER TWO

MOTHER'S WONDERFUL
IDEA

AND NOW, the little family was going to have to live through one of the bitterest winters ever. Worst of all, it had started so terribly early. By November, their little house, high on the slope, was nearly buried in the deep white drifts of snow, and the Mother and her children could barely step out of their door. Barty and Franzeli played in their corner close to the stove, for they could not go outside any more.

Once in a while, when there was no bread left in the house at all, the Mother would have to brave the winter weather and go down to the village. The snow had piled up so thick and deep that it was almost impossible to get down the steep hill. There was no path except when the one lonely man who lived even higher up on the slope made one on his way to the village. The Mother would look for his footprints to step into whenever she had to go out. But if it had been snowing again, then she would have to force her own way through the deep drifts. Returning home on these days, she was so weary that she could scarcely keep herself on her feet. Yet there was so much to do that she could not allow herself to rest until much later.

Still, it was not her weariness that made her sit so silent and sad when, at last, late in the evening, she set about mending her children's clothes. Her worries were growing with each wintry day. Often she did not know how she could buy even a small loaf of bread, for there were many times when she could not find work.

Once there had been a whole week in which she had not earned a penny from her knitting. Then there had been no bread, and the small amount of milk they got from their skinny goat was all the food there was for the three of them.

Yet, to go to the village authorities for help was out of the question. For they would have separated the children and sent each child to live with a different family. And the Mother felt that her little family would be better off to face anything together, rather than to agree to such a cruel separation.

That was the reason why the Mother sat and worried during the long nights about ways to earn even a small amount of money, for there were still three hard winter months ahead of them. In happier times, when she had tucked the little ones into their beds and sat beside them with her patchwork or knitting, she had hummed a song and the children had dropped off to sleep listening to her. Now the Mother sat there silently and sadly, and no song would come to her unsmiling lips.

One December evening, the Mother was very worried. Outside, the mountain winds were howling around the little house, shaking and rattling it as if they meant to blow it down into the valley. Franzeli had curled up and fallen asleep immediately in spite of the wind's frightful whistling and moaning. For she had nothing to fear as long as her brother and Mother were close by. But Barty kept his eyes wide open, watching his Mother as she bent over her mending.

Suddenly, he asked, "Mother, why don't you sing to us any more?"

"Goodness!" she replied with a start. "I thought you both were sleeping!" Then she shook her head sadly. "I have forgotten all about singing," she said softly.

"Don't you know the songs any more?" asked Barty as he sat straight up in bed. "Wait, I'll sing one for you!" and he began to sing:

Night is falling darkly now,
Spreading over hill and wood,
All His children pray to God
To bless them and to make them good.

With a clear steady voice the little boy finished the song that he had heard his Mother sing on so many evenings. As she listened with pleasure, suddenly a wonderful idea came to her. Hugging the boy to her joyfully, she exclaimed, "Barty! God has just sent me an idea. You can help me to earn bread again for you and Franzeli. You'd like to do that, wouldn't you?"

"Oh, yes, yes! I want to!" And Barty clapped his hands. "Right now?" he asked, and started immediately to climb out of bed.

"No, no, go back to bed again," laughed the Mother. "Look, how you are shivering!" And she quickly pulled the blanket up over the little boy. "Not now, but tomorrow I will teach you a song, a Christmas Carol, and on Christmas Day you may sing it for the people in the village. They will give you bread, and perhaps even nuts and Christmas goodies."

The thought of these gifts and, best of all, his important part in earning them, excited Barty so that he squirmed about under his warm blanket.

Now he did not have to keep his eyes open. They refused to shut. After a few minutes, he called out, "Mother! Is it morning yet?"

"No, dear," said his Mother, shaking her head in amusement as she continued her mending.

The blanket humped and rolled and twisted, and soon Barty's voice called out again. "Mother, will it *ever* be tomorrow?"

"Soon enough, soon enough," answered his mother.

Again the blanket became very active as Barty wiggled with excitement at the thought of singing his carol in the village. He could just imagine the basketful of good things he would get for Mother and for Franzeli, if only the morning would come. But the blanket lay still at last, because Barty was quiet under it. Sleep had come long before the morning.

As the Mother finished her mending, she noticed that the wind had died down, and the only sound in the small still hut was the breathing of the two sleeping children, and her own soft humming. She had been happy enough to start singing again without realizing it.

CHAPTER THREE

THE CHILDREN
LEARN A SONG

THE NEXT MORNING, Barty awoke with a bounce. He remembered the wonderful idea. At last the morning had arrived, and today Mother would teach him the Christmas song. When Barty was dressed, he stood before his Mother, his face smiling and eager. "I'm ready to begin," he announced gaily.

His Mother, busy with one of her many tasks, stopped long enough to pat the golden head. "Be patient a little longer," she said, smiling at the boy. "We won't be able to do our singing before tonight." The child's face clouded. "Well, Barty, you can see how much work I have to do today. But this evening, I shall sit down with my knitting and with you, and then we'll start our carol."

Barty forced himself to be content with that, and it helped the long day pass when he told Franzeli about their Mother's plan. "And I shall go from house to house," Barty told the little girl, "singing the beautiful song Mother will teach me. And most wonderful of all, Franzeli, Do you know what?" Franzeli could only shake her head silently. "*Then*," said Barty proudly, "After I sing, everyone will give me things in my

Christmas basket. Bread, maybe even a few nuts, for a Chistmas treat, and we shall all have a lovely feast afterwards!"

"Oh, Barty," breathed the little girl. "I can't wait for the evening to come, too."

When the early December dusk had fallen, darkening the mountains and the sky, Mother finished her work. She lit the little lamp and asked the two watching children to sit down at the table beside her, Barty close on one side and Franzeli snuggled against the other. Then she started working on the warm socks for Barty which had to be knitted in time for him to wear them on his Christmas adventure.

The knitting needles clicked and the old rocker squeaked comfortably. "Now listen to me, Barty," said the Mother. "I will sing you the first verse a few times. Then you join me and we'll see whether you know it." The Mother sang, and soon Barty joined her in his steady sweet voice. Suddenly, Franzeli, whose lips had been moving silently while the others sang, softly added her voice to theirs.

The Mother nodded encouragingly, and said when they reached the end of the verse, "Good, Franzeli. Perhaps some day you will learn the song, too." After the Mother had sung the first verse over and over and over again, she asked, "Do you want to try it now, Barty? Franzeli will help you a little, won't you?" The little girl nodded delightedly, and Barty started singing with a steady rhythm.

To the Mother's amazement, Franzeli joined in with a voice as pure and true as the tinkling of silver bells. The Mother had not noticed it when the three of them were all singing together. And whenever Barty had a little trouble staying with the tune, Franzeli continued to sing right on. "She's like a little bird," her Mother thought, "that finishes its melody without effort and without mistake."

The Mother was pleased beyond words. She never had thought that Franzeli could help, but the two children singing together were remarkably good. They sounded so lovely that the Mother leaned her head back in the rocking chair and just listened. The two little voices pleased her more than anything she had ever heard before.

From that night on, they sang every evening. By the week's end they knew all four verses of the song, and could sing it through without hesitation.

Barty and Franzeli were so thrilled to have learned their own special Christmas Carol that they couldn't get enough of it. Over and over and over, they sang their carol in the long days they were forced to spend indoors. Hearing them, the Mother felt comfortable and content. She knew that the children would not forget the words in the middle of the song even if she herself were not there to help them. They seemed really sure of the entire song now.

On the last evening before Christmas, the Mother practiced one more time with the children to make sure they knew the song perfectly. They sang with such eagerness and spirit that the Mother found herself singing joyously along with them.

Without hesitation, and with true feeling they sang the four verses of their Christmas Carol:

THE CHILDREN'S CHRISTMAS CAROL

The old year is nearly over,
And Christmas time is here;
May your heart be filled with gladness,
And your home with warmth and cheer.

Chill winter and its whistling wind
With ice has bound the land;
But never fear, for God is near:
He'll lead you by the hand.

The winter birds now find it hard
To get their food each day;
And even little children, too,
For daily bread do pray.

But still this snowy Christmas time
Reminds us, in the end,
That we will always have His help
Who choose God for our friend.

CHAPTER FOUR

THE CHRISTMAS CAROL

IT WAS Christmas morning. The pealing of the church bells down in the village rang in the clear, cold air and echoed from the mountainside.

Franzeli and Barty were dressed in their warmest clothes, and each wore a new pair of heavy knitted stockings that was their Mother's Christmas present to them. Barty's were dark green and Franzeli's were red. The children loved them not just because they were warm and bright, but because they had watched their Mother knit them with love and care.

The excited children found it hard to wait for their big adventure. But finally Mother was ready, bringing a small basket for Barty to carry and an old shawl of hers which she put around Franzeli.

The snow was too deep for a little girl to walk in, so the Mother picked Franzeli up in her arms and said the words they had been waiting to hear: "Now we can go." Barty led, bravely working his way step by step through the deep snow until they reached the road that ran alongside the Schachen Brook.

Here he could walk side by side with his Mother, and even Franzeli could be put down at last. The sky overhead was brilliantly blue, and the mountain peaks sparkled as though they had been powdered with diamond dust. The merry pealing of the bells echoed and re-echoed until the air seemed alive with their sound. Barty and Franzeli were amused at the way the snow squeaked under foot, and they laughed aloud to see the little puffs of cloud that appeared before them every time they breathed or spoke in the frosty air. For they did not often get out in this weather.

The walk down to the village was filled with such wonders that the time flew by, and almost an hour had passed without their realizing it.

When they reached the first houses of Altdorf, the Mother saw that many children were already on their way to sing Christmas Carols, going in and out of every house. So the little family went on until they reached the big Inn. This part of the village was still rather quiet.

There, under the snow-trimmed sign of the Golden Eagle, the little family stopped. Mother straightened the children's caps, gave them each a hug, and told them to start singing as soon as they entered the Inn. She herself remained outside, half hidden behind a tree, but standing where she could have a view of the front entrance when the children came out.

Barty, acting much braver than he really felt, took Franzeli's hand and led her boldly toward the Inn. The children opened the heavy front door, and gasped at the sight that greeted them.

A huge fire crackled cheerily in the largest fireplace either child had ever seen. There were many soft chairs and couches on which the guests sat, scattered around the big main room. But what really caught the children's attention was a large table in the center of the room. On it was a bowl the size of Mother's wash tub, and it was filled to over-flowing with bright colored fruits and good brown nuts.

With their eyes nearly popping out of their heads, the two little ones stood with their backs against the door, and remembering their Mother's instructions, they began to sing at once.

Barty's clear voice rang out, and Franzeli's chimed in sweetly. As the words carried across the big room the guests became quiet. They motioned to the singing children to come closer, and without missing a beat the brother and sister moved forward hand in hand, singing.

It was fortunate that they had learned their carol so well, for they sang it now almost without thinking. They walked forward in a daze, their wondering eyes never leaving the bowl of luscious fruits.

When the last verse was finished the guests applauded warmly. "Well done!" "Beautiful!" "What lovely voices!" they cried. Barty's little basket was taken from him, and when it was returned it held rolls and bread and even a few silver coins.

"Oh, thank you," the children murmured. "Thank you and a Merry
Christmas!" Just then the innkeeper's wife bustled over to them. "On
Christmas Day you have to have something special with your bread,"
she said smiling broadly. And she took several shiny red apples and two
whole handfuls of nuts and piled them into the basket, too.

"Thank you, thank you," Barty said, loudly and clearly this time,
while Franzeli repeated it timidly after him. Then, enchanted with
their gifts, the children ran out to show the partly filled basket to their
Mother.

The children walked on with their Mother along the little village street, stopping at each house on the way. Sometimes they found that there was already quite a group of children singing their carols at a house. Once, when that happened, a man came to the door with bread for everyone, saying, "My wife and I would rather give a piece of bread to each of you than listen to so much noise!" But he said it with a twinkle in his eyes, and the children took their bread and moved on, giggling about the gruff joke.

Sometimes, when there was a large group of carolers, not all of them got something, and a few had to leave empty-handed.

However, once, when many children stood in front of a door, the woman called little Franzeli over, saying, "Come, you little one. You are almost freezing to death. You have to get something, but then you must hurry home. Because, look, you are shivering like a leaf."

After the children had sung in seven or eight houses, their Mother saw that they could not go on much longer. It was so bitterly cold that she herself was very chilled, and delicate little Franzeli could scarcely sing for the chattering of her teeth. Even sturdy Barty's cheeks were turning red with the cold.

"Come, children," said the Mother. "We'll walk fast so you can get warm again." They walked as briskly as they could all the long uphill way to their tiny house. There, all three of them huddled close to each other around the little stove till their hands and feet were warm once more. But the thought of the good things to eat in their basket warmed them almost as much as their stove.

Then, at last, Barty fetched the little basket and they unpacked its treasures. Bread and rolls enough to last them many days! And the coins that would buy them even more food! But best of all were the nuts and glowing red apples—treats the children had seldom eaten in their hungry lives.

So they celebrated a gay Christmas, each with a large soft roll, some nuts and a slice of delicious crisp apple. Mother, too, was happy and grateful. She had enough food and money now to take care of them for some time. The days were beginning to get longer again, and the world was turning toward spring. Somehow, with God's help, they would get through the winter. She sang softly, hopefully:

> *But still this snowy Christmas time*
> *Reminds us, in the end,*
> *That we will always have His help*
> *Who choose God for our friend.*

CHAPTER FIVE

SUMMER IN THE ALPS

FINALLY the long winter came to an end. Even after their wonderful Christmas, there had been difficult days when the weather was freezing and the cupboard was empty. But they had managed somehow. The Mother would get an order to knit a pair of socks or mittens and there would be money for food again, just in the nick of time.

And now it was summer and the sunshine was warm. The cottage door stood open all day long, and the children played on the sweet smelling meadow in front of the house. The goat, too, was freed from its cramped winter stable and taken outdoors to graze on the young tender grass. Its skinny body had filled out, and it gave more milk, and richer milk as well.

The Mother still had a great deal to do. She was out from morning till night looking all over for wood and carrying it home so they would have a supply to heat the little house the next winter.

And though the sun shone warmly and the air was mild, the Mother sometimes trembled with weakness. She had worked too hard and eaten too little through the hard winter, and her strength seemed to have left her now. But she went right on with her difficult tasks. She was afraid that if she were no longer able to take care of herself and the children properly, the family would be separated and the children sent away. This was such a terrible thought that the Mother struggled on with all her remaining strength to keep her little family together.

But the children, rejoicing in the long, hot summer days, knew nothing of their Mother's troubles. They wandered hand in hand through the green meadows sprinkled with wildflowers. Each day they picked a fresh bouquet and brought it back to brighten the little house.

One morning, when the sun burned down from a cloudless sky, the Mother said, "This is the day for gathering our hay. You children may come along with me and help." The brother and sister skipped about like playful mountain goats. To go along with Mother higher up the mountainside was a big treat. They always took their small share of bread and had a picnic high up above the world.

The three of them climbed up the steep slope to a small piece of ground that lay behind a large rock. Here, year after year, the Mother had harvested this little patch of grass for winter food for the goat. The day before, she had cut the grass and laid it out on the mountainside to dry.

The hot sun had done its job well. The grass was dry and brittle and smelled of warmth and sunshine and sweet summer air. Barty scooped up a fragrant armload and he and Franzeli buried their faces in the hay. But it prickled and tickled, and with much sneezing they soon got down to the business of helping their Mother tie the hay up in bundles.

The Mother took the largest bundle and carried it down the mountain on her head. Franzeli, as she always did if Mother could not hold her hand, followed close at her Mother's heels, clutching at her skirt. And Barty brought up the last of this small procession, proudly carrying a smaller load of warm, dry hay on his head.

It was five o'clock in the afternoon when they reached home, and the mountain was already throwing a long shadow. The precious hay was carefully stowed in the loft of the tiny goat shed. Then Mother fetched them each a bowl of milk, for they had had nothing but their small picnic lunch all day, and the exercise had made them hungry.

It was not until the Mother went to the cupboard to take out the loaf of bread that she noticed what a very little piece was left. She would not be getting any more money to buy bread with until she finished knitting the socks that she would sell. And because of the haymaking during the past few days she had not had time to knit.

For one dreadful moment, the Mother wanted to give up. But instead she squared her tired shoulders and lifted her chin. Then, dividing the small piece of bread into two pieces, she gave half to Franzeli and half to Barty, saying, "I know how hungry you must be after your day of haying, but see, children, I've only this to give you with your cheese. But tonight I shall get a lot of knitting done, and tomorrow there will be more food, and a big piece of bread for each of you."

Barty took his small chunk of bread cheerfully, but halfway to his mouth his hand paused, and he waited before starting to eat. He watched his Mother pouring milk into their bowls and then sitting down and resting her head in her hands. "Where is your bread, Mother?" the boy asked.

"I have none, Barty," his Mother told him. "But I'm not hungry. I don't need anything."

"Yes, you do!" It was Franzeli who had stopped eating when she heard her Mother say this. Running over to her Mother, Franzeli put the tiny piece of bread she still had left into her Mother's mouth. Barty held out his portion, too, and said in a voice of distress, "But if you don't have any bread you'll have to go hungry, so we'll share."

But his Mother gently pushed his hand back. "No, no, Barty. You eat this. I really couldn't eat anyhow. I don't feel very well." Then she said in a low voice, as if to herself, "If only I could go down to Altdorf tomorrow and see a doctor. I can't go on like this." And stumbling over to her bed, she sank down on it. She was so weak and tired she had fainted.

Barty regarded her solemnly for a little while. She must have fallen asleep, he thought. The boy was deeply puzzled, but suddenly a wonderful idea came to him, his face brightened and he turned to his little sister. "Come on, Franzeli," he whispered. "I know what we will do. But you mustn't make any noise. We don't want to wake Mother. See, she just needs to sleep a little."

With that he took Franzeli's small hand in his and pulled her to the open door. The children couldn't help but move noiselessly, for neither of them wore shoes or stockings. Quietly they tiptoed out the door and started down the mountainside together.

After they had passed the steep foot path down the slope and were walking beside the rushing brook, Barty pushed Franzeli away from the water to the other side of the path. "You had better walk 'way over on the far side of the path, Franzeli," he warned her. "You see, if you walk too close to the Schachen Brook you could fall in. It is so wild and deep here that Mother says a little child like you could drown." Franzeli understood that and quickly moved over even further until she was walking in the meadow.

Barty continued, feeling very grown up and responsible. "Look, Franzeli, we are going to Altdorf to sing our Christmas Carol again. It is the only thing we can do, and perhaps we will get bread and maybe even some nuts like we did the last time. Then we'll take it all back to Mother for a surprise, because she has had no bread today."

Franzeli nodded happily. She did not have the breath to shout above the roaring of the brook.

"Do you still know the song?" Barty asked.

Franzeli answered by starting to sing it, and Barty joined in. Over and over again, all the way to the village, the children sang their song. The long hard walk had made Franzeli tired, but as they had come to the first houses in the village she was too excited to notice.

They stopped their singing as Barty looked around. "I still remember very well where to start," he said. "It is not here. No. It is a little further on." And he pulled Franzeli, who was getting more and more tired, along the cobbled street to the large Inn. Yes, there was the sign of the Golden Eagle, but how different it looked now without its trimming of snow and icicles.

The red-gold rays of the evening sun gilded the small courtyard in front of the entrance door. The children stopped for a moment, made shy by the sound of sudden laughter and voices coming from the other side of the hedge. They looked at each other questioningly. What could all that noise mean?

CHAPTER SIX

CHRISTMAS IN AUGUST

ON THE OTHER side of the hedge a gay party was in progress. A group of American students who were taking a bicycle tour through Switzerland had arrived that afternoon. The six young men were in high spirits and had asked the innkeeper to serve them their supper out of doors. They had carried the big heavy table from the Inn's main room and set it out in the courtyard. There, in the slanting rays of the August afternoon sun, with the purple-shadowed mountains towering above them, they laughed and talked and ate. They were happy to relax after the day's bicycling.

Barty and Franzeli peeked around the hedge. Seeing so many noisy men dressed in strange clothing, Franzeli started to pull back, but Barty held her hand firmly. "We had better start singing from here," he told her. "And *loud*, or they'll never hear us over their own noise." So the two children stood at the opening in the hedge and began to sing their carol as loudly as they could.

One of the young men tapped his spoon against his glass. "Quiet!" he said in English. "I think I hear somebody singing. Maybe we're going to have dinner music!" The other students all looked around, and, seeing the two children who stood half hidden behind the hedge, they called them over.

The children stopped singing, and Barty, who did not understand, said in German, "What is it, please?"

"Come on, come closer. Come over here," one of the students called in German.

"Oh," Barty replied. "But gladly," and he started toward the table eagerly. But Franzeli was afraid, and he had to tug at her a bit to make her follow.

A tall young man with very red hair and a deep suntan reached out with his long arm and drew Barty still closer to the table. "Well, youngsters," he smiled at them. "Now sing your song. Be brave!"

Barty sang very loudly and little Franzeli joined in with her voice like a soft silver bell:

The old year is nearly over,
And Christmas time is here.
May your heart be filled with gladness,
And your home with warmth and cheer.

"Fellows, if my German is correct," the tall red-haired man said, "they're celebrating Christmas over here today!"

"Yes," broke in another student. "Switzerland—the upside down country. They celebrate Christmas in August!"

At this, such shouts and whoops of laughter went up from the whole table that the startled children stopped singing.

"Now look what you've done, Red," said a man with curly dark hair. "You and your noisy jokes—you've made the little girl shake like a leaf."

The students became quiet and they all looked at Franzeli clinging timidly to her brother.

"All right, Doc," Red told the dark-haired man. "You take care of little Goldilocks here, and let us get on with the song."

Doc took Franzeli's hand with great tenderness, and said in German, "You come to me, little girl, and nobody will hurt you. I have a sister about your size back in America."

Franzeli took his large warm hand trustingly, and as soon as everyone settled down quietly, Barty continued the carol:

> *Chill winter and its whistling wind*
> *With ice has bound the land;*
> *But never fear, for God is near:*
> *He'll lead you by the hand.*

"We certainly didn't have to worry about freezing in this August sunshine!" Red interrupted as he pointed to his sunburned face. Again laughter rang out around the table, but this time the children smiled, too, though they still were not certain what the joke was. The students shouted encouragingly, "Go on, go on! Sing the rest." So Barty and Franzeli took a deep breath and went on:

The winter birds now find it hard
To get their food each day;
And even little children, too,
For daily bread do pray.

The children could not help staring hungrily at the platters of delicious food while they sang this last verse. Some of the young men must have noticed, because they called out, "These youngsters have to get something to eat!" And plates heaped with all kinds of wonderful food were pushed toward the children.

Those two brave little ones, though tempted, merely swallowed hard and went right on singing their carol:

But still this snowy Christmas time
Reminds us, in the end,
That we will always have His help
Who choose God for our friend.

There was great merriment mixed with the applause that followed. Some of the students blew on their hands and slapped their bare arms, pretending to be cold on this mild August evening.

"So it's Christmas here in Switzerland, eh?" they said, laughing heartily. "Well, then, you must have your Christmas dinner!" And Red heaped up more good things on Barty's plate. There was more food than the little boy had seen in all his life before. Sausages and other meats and different kinds of cheese and a big piece of white bread were all heaped up together on a huge platter.

"Come on, son," Red said encouragingly. "Go to work bravely, and don't stop till you've eaten it all." The others took tempting morsels from their dishes and passed those to Barty, too. "Take this also," they urged.

Barty just stood there looking at these riches, his eyes bright with delight and growing bigger every minute. But he didn't touch a thing.

Franzeli still clung to the hand of her protector, and she, too, had

a full plate put in front of her. "Here's your Christmas dinner, little girl," someone told her jokingly. "Go ahead and eat it." Franzeli was very hungry after her long walk and she took a good sized piece of meat on her fork and was just about to put it in her mouth when she glanced over to Barty first to see if it was all right. But noticing that he was not touching his food yet, she put her fork quickly back on the plate.

"What's the matter, boy? Why don't you eat?" Red asked the boy. "And by the way, what is your name?"

"My name is Sebastian, but they call me Barty."

"Well, Barty, my friend. What are you thinking about so seriously that you can't eat? Is there something else you want?"

"Yes," Barty answered. "If I only had a sack!"

"A sack?" They all looked at the boy. "What would you do with a sack?"

"I want to put everything in it and take it to my Mother," Barty explained. "She hasn't had anything to eat all day."

The students looked at one another, suddenly serious. Then gently they began to question the boy.

"Where do your parents live?"

"My Father lives up in Heaven," Barty said simply. "And Mother lives about half way up the mountain there." And he pointed behind him.

The students whistled and murmured in amazement. Red said, "But Barty, if you and your little sister came all the way down from there you must be starving—aren't you?"

"Well, yes," Barty admitted, while Franzeli nodded her head vigorously. "Especially because we had only a very little piece of bread today. But tomorrow Mother may get paid for the socks she knit and then we shall have more. Poor Mother had nothing at all today."

The young men looked at one another as if they couldn't believe what they had heard. There was so much food on their own table, it was hard to imagine anyone could starve within miles of Altdorf. Suddenly they decided they must all do something to help these children.

Several students rushed into the Inn to get paper bags. Two more went in search of their knapsacks where they had bars of chocolate and dried fruit.

But Doc clapped his hands together and announced, "First of all I want to see these children eat until they aren't one bit hungry any more, then we can decide what to do next. Listen Barty, and you little Franzeli, you eat everything on your plates, and after you've finished we'll see that your Mother gets all the rest of the food that's on the table."

"All this?" Barty asked, his eyes shining as he pointed to the heaping platters.

"Everything!" Doc and Red both answered. Then Red asked, "Will you start eating now, under those conditions?"

For answer, Barty seized his fork and he ate with such enjoyment that Red and Doc and the others leaned back and watched him with smiles of satisfaction. Franzeli, too, began to eat her dinner, and small and delicate though she was, she soon made the pile of good things on her plate grow smaller and then disappear altogether.

Once in a while, the students interrupted the hungry children with a question.

"Did your Mother send you out to sing the Christmas Carol?" Red asked after a thoughtful silence.

"Oh, no," Barty replied, wiping his mouth with the back of his hand. "She fell asleep because she hadn't eaten and she was tired. So I took Franzeli to get some bread for Mother, so that she would have something to eat when she woke up! Because the first time we sang here we got some bread and nuts and apples, last Christmas."

Now the students understood how it happened that the children had sung them a Christmas Carol on an August evening. And they were all a little sheepish at the way they had first acted.

"Well, now," said Red, clearing his throat and trying to speak lightly, though it was plain to see that he, too, was moved. "I suggest we accompany our singers to their home. We were going up the mountain tomorrow anyhow to see the place in the Schachen Brook where William Tell was drowned. We'll see it by moonlight instead, and deliver our friends to their Mother at the same time."

"Good idea!" said Doc. Turning to Barty, he explained, "I just graduated from medical school, and I'd like to see your Mother. Maybe I can help her."

Everyone was on his feet and ready to leave when the innkeeper's wife hurried out of the front door and over to the table with a huge basket. "The young men asked me for sacks, but that won't do," she said severely. Barty looked miserable. She was not going to let them take the food to Mother after all, he thought. How sorry he was that he had eaten all of his! Now there would be nothing to bring home.

The woman went to work clearing the table, and her capable hands soon had the cheeses and sausages and bread packed neatly into the basket. "It wouldn't have been nice to throw all this food any old way into sacks," she muttered. "Let's see, there's still more room." And she scurried back into the Inn, returning in a few minutes with her apron filled with apples, potatoes and even a bunch of grapes. She was packing the basket for *them*, Barty realized, and he was so happy he could have hugged the innkeeper's wife.

The students started to thank her, but she said sharply, "It's so things will be packed firmly and won't slide around in the basket."

"Let's go!" called Red. Two of the boys carried a long stick between them with the basket slung over it. Doc hoisted Franzeli to his shoulders. "She can't walk all that way a second time when it is so late," he explained.

But Barty proudly led the way with Red. His confidence in his new friend had grown so great that, all the way up to the little hut, he chattered on and on about how they lived at home, the three of them and the goat, and about the ordinary adventures of their daily life. He could not know that, to Red, it was one of the greatest tales of bravery and love that he had ever heard. Barty did wonder though, why such a young man had to stop to rest and mop his face so often. Maybe in America that was the way they were.

CHAPTER SEVEN

HELPING HANDS

IT HAD grown nearly dark in the little house when at last the Mother stirred on her bed. She lifted her head from the pillow and tried to get up, but she lacked the strength, and she fell back weakly.

Again and again, the Mother fought against the dizziness and weakness, until finally she was able to sit up on the edge of her bed. In the darkness of the little room she could not see her children, and then she realized that it was completely silent outside as well as indoors. Where could the children be?

"Barty! Franzeli!" the Mother called as loudly as she was able. But though she listened carefully, not a sound came to her from the darkness. Then fear gave her strength. She got up quickly and felt her way to the square of dusky light that shone through the open door.

Nobody was outside. She looked into the stable and saw only the goat, who raised her white head, hopeful that this was a new feeding time. All around the small house the Mother walked, calling her children at every step. But there was no answer. The only sound that came

to her straining ears was the roaring of the Schachen Brook down below.

A horrible fear came over the Mother, and the sound of the raging water seemed to grow louder. She leaned against the rough wall of the little house, clasping her hands and praying with all her heart that no harm had come to the children. Then she ran over to the foot path and started down the mountain toward the Brook.

It was then that she saw a band of people climbing toward her. She could hear loud and eager voices, and it seemed as though the shadowy shapes were pointing toward her little house. "Oh, good Lord in Heaven!" she moaned. "Are they bringing bad news to me?" And the Mother stood there so frightened that she could not move.

"Mother! Mother!" It was Barty's voice floating up on the clear air and echoing back from the mountain. "We are coming! We are coming! And wait till you see what we are bringing you!"

And soon there was Barty, running ahead of the others, shouting and talking breathlessly, trying to tell his Mother everything that had happened all at once. Long before the Mother could understand just what had taken place, Barty had flung himself into her waiting arms. She could only hug her son and thank God with all her heart that her children were safe. When she looked beyond Barty at the group making its way up the steep path, with Franzeli sitting high on the shoulders of

a tall young man, she suddenly realized that something out of the ordinary was taking place.

Even in the moonlight, the Mother could see that these were strange young men, and not from the village. As they drew close she could tell from their clothes and their voices that they were not even from this land. Yet there was her timid little Franzeli happily riding on the shoulders of one of the men and talking and laughing as she would to her Mother.

By this time the American students had reached the Mother, who stood with one arm around Barty's shoulder.

"Hello, there, Mother," they greeted her, as if she were an old friend. "We hope you are feeling better now." The man who was carrying Franzeli set her down in front of her Mother. "Here's your daughter safe and sound," he said. "And weighing several more pounds than she did on her way down the mountain!" And he reached out and shook the Mother's hand. "Oh, Mother," Franzeli told her, "they have been so good to us. See what they have brought you," and she pointed to the heavy basket slung on the pole between two of the young men.

Nothing would do but that Barty and Franzeli bring their new friends up to the little house in spite of the lateness of the hour. When the six large young men trooped into the small room, it seemed as though the very walls bulged. The Mother lit their one small lamp, and Red, who could barely stand at his full height under the low ceiling, sat down in the doorway with his long legs outside.

Since Red was the tallest, the Mother took him to be the leader of the group, and she thanked him over and over again for the marvelous things the children were unpacking from the basket. There was more, much more, than the tiny cupboard could hold. It seemed impossible that its well-stocked shelves could ever be empty again.

"We heard you weren't feeling well," Red told the Mother, "so we brought you a doctor, too." And he introduced Doc. The Mother recognized the kind young man who had carried Franzeli up the mountain.

"While you talk to him, the rest of us can go outside and admire your view of the mountains. It is a rare sight for us to see an Alpine house and these mountains in the moonlight."

Barty led them outdoors. "And you must see our goat, too," he cried joyfully. The poor goat was not used to being disturbed so often in the night, and this time she bleated in disappointment at only being admired and not fed. "Very well," said Barty as he pulled down a few wisps of new hay from the loft. "But that will mean so much the less for you this winter." Red and the others exchanged meaningful looks over the little boy's head.

Inside the house, the Mother was telling Doc that she had no pains to complain of, only a terrible weakness. Gently he asked her what she usually had to eat, and when she told him truthfully he nodded his head several times.

"Mother," he said, "I am going to speak to your village doctor in the morning, and if he agrees he'll see that you get a certain excellent tonic that I know of."

The Mother thanked him with tears in her eyes. "No, no, don't thank me," the young man said. "Because you can do something for me, too. For all of us, in fact. Wait till the others come in and we'll tell you what we want."

The Mother nodded, but she wondered what she could possibly do for these young men. What could they possibly want that she could give them from this poor bare house of hers?

When the others returned and arranged themselves comfortably on the floor, Red spoke up. "Mother," he said, "Barty and Franzeli have been telling us that you knit some of the most beautiful socks and sweaters and scarves in the whole village."

The Mother became very embarrassed and said modestly that she did knit a little, but nothing fine, such as they could buy in stores in America, she was sure.

"But that's just it," one of the others spoke up. "It is very difficult and very expensive to find things knitted by hand in American stores. Only the very rich can afford them."

This the Mother found hard to believe, but she was too polite to argue about it.

"We were wondering," Red continued. "How long does it take you to knit a pair of socks, for example?"

"Oh," the Mother said after a moment's thought, "if I have time I can do them in two or three days."

"And a scarf?"

"About three days. A sweater in a week or so."

"Mm, hm," Red took out a notebook and pencil. "And what do you charge?" he asked, very businesslike. The Mother told him, and he wrote the figures down. Then he figured some more and looked up seriously.

"If we ordered anything to be made by you we would have to add on some extra for postage to America, for wrapping the package, and for your time in taking it to the village to be mailed."

The Mother smiled and agreed. Such funny games these grown-up Americans liked to play. It was like the games that Barty and Franzeli played endlessly on rainy days. So she played their game with them patiently. Her two children were watching and listening with eyes aglow, and mouths open. Children, all of them, she thought.

The Mother never did quite know when it was that the game had turned real. But all at once she found herself with measurements and colors for six pairs of socks and six woolen scarves, and six addresses to mail them to in the United States. And at her elbow on the table, an unbelievable pile of money lay in the lamplight.

Red was talking. "We won't get home ourselves till next month, so there's no hurry. We won't need the socks and scarves until November when it turns cold. And when we do get home we're going to take orders for our families for Christmas, so you can count on keeping your knitting needles busy from now on."

When the Mother at last had recovered from her surprise, she tried once more to thank the students. But they waved her thanks aside gaily, shook her hand and kissed the children goodnight.

" 'Way past bed-time," said Doc, looking at his watch. "Take care of yourself, now."

Barty and Franzeli ran from one to another of their departing guests. "Come back again soon!" they begged.

"Maybe next year, Barty, my friend!" Red promised over his shoulder. Barty and Franzeli stood in front of their house waving, and Barty called, "Thank you all, and God bless you all!" And the moonlit mountains echoed back his words.

CHAPTER EIGHT

A VERY MERRY
CHRISTMAS

ONCE AGAIN, the meadow and mountains and the little house and stable were thickly frosted with snow. Once again crystal icicles hung from the roof and Christmas was in the air.

But this year how different it was! The Mother had worked busily indoors most of the time. The click of her knitting needles and the creaking of her rocking chair had made a pleasant background for their talk and songs. And oh! How they talked and sang! For there was no longer the gloom of worry to darken the little family's days.

The Mother's cheeks were as pink as Barty's, and the new tonic had restored her strength. The orders she kept getting from the American students brought her more money than she had ever dared dream of. Now the cupboard held loaves of good bread, sausage, and sometimes even fruit. And the goat gave plenty of milk in December, too. For she was kept fat and sleek on a plentiful diet of extra hay that had been bought for her.

Barty and Franzeli sat at their Mother's feet and sang Christmas Carols. This year they had learned three new ones, but the old one was still their favorite.

"Shall we go down to the village to sing our Christmas Carols again this year?" Barty asked.

"We want to so much," little Franzeli coaxed.

"I don't know," the Mother said doubtfully. "Remember how cold we all were last year. But then it had been necessary—we had no other way to get bread. This year we can sing our carols up here and God will listen and hear them just as well." The Mother's eyes twinkled, "And perhaps if your singing is very good I may give you some bread and nuts."

"Oh!" The children were disappointed, but they could see that their Mother was right. They still did not own sturdy warm boots and heavy winter coats to wear outdoors in the cold. They did not mind having to stay indoors and having to play near the stove most of the winter, but they had hoped against hope for a Christmas outing like last year's.

"Well," said the Mother in order to change the subject, "do you suppose your American friends have had your Christmas greetings yet?"

"Oh, I hope they'll like the picture of our house and the mountains in winter. I can't draw very well," Barty spoke apologetically, "but they can see how different it looks now."

"Do you think Doc will like the meadow flowers I pressed for him?" asked Franzeli anxiously. Since she had no father she had given her love to the stranger who had been so kind to her. "Do you suppose they think of us far away in America as often as we think of them?" the little girl added in a wistful voice.

"I'm sure they do sometimes," their Mother said. "But they are all busy young men, and they don't have as much time as we do for such things."

The short December days passed quickly and before they knew it, it was the day before Christmas. That morning, they were greately astonished to hear a loud knocking on the door. No one ever came up the mountain in all that snow, and the children and their Mother looked at one another wonderingly.

Carefully, the Mother went to the door and opened it a tiny crack. There stood the mailman mopping his forehead in spite of the cold, and at his feet lay a huge package that he had evidently struggled up the mountain to deliver.

"This has your name on it," he said, "but are you expecting such a large package?"

"Not I," the mother told him. "You must have come to the wrong place with your big box. I'm sorry."

"Read for yourself," the mailman replied with a shrug.

As a matter of fact, all of their names and the address were clearly written on the label. "Why it comes from America!" the Mother exclaimed.

"Just what I thought," said the postman, scratching his head. "There must be some mistake."

But Barty and Franzeli were jumping up and down by this time. "No mistake!" Barty yelled. "It is from our American friends!"

"Yes! Yes!" cried Franzeli who was quite beside herself. "They have not forgotten us!"

"Glad I don't have to take it back then," said the postman. "Merry Christmas!" And with a wave of his hand, he was off, following his own footsteps back through the snow.

The Mother and children opened the package with eager fingers. Barty sniffed like a little dog when the lid was lifted from the box. "I think I can smell the American air still in here," he explained seriously.

But Mother and Franzeli were exclaiming over the other things in the box. There was a heavy blue coat for a girl Franzeli's size, and a warm ski jacket and trousers that would just fit Barty. There were two pairs of fleece-lined boots for children, and another pair in a woman's size, two red and white striped canes that smelled like peppermint candy— Franzeli touched one with the tip of her tongue and it *was* peppermint candy!—and at the very bottom of the box lay a square card. Mother picked it up and read it aloud. It said:

> *But still this snowy Christmas time*
> *Reminds us, in the end,*
> *That we will always have His help*
> *Who choose God for our friend.*

And on the other side:

This was as true in August as it is in December. Merry Christmas from your American friends.

"This is a blessing, a blessing!" the Mother said, clasping her hands.

"Those words are from our Christmas Carol!" Barty exclaimed. "And now we can sing our carol in the village tomorrow after all! Mother, we will all be quite warm enough this year!"

"Yes, indeed," the Mother agreed. "Blessedly warm. And you are right, children. We should sing our carol for everyone in Altdorf tomorrow."

Then she took the card that had come in the package, and carefully she hung it on the wall above their table. Putting her arms around the two children, she stood looking at it. "That is so all the year long we will remember our Friend," she said. "And also our friends," she added.

And they never forgot, for many, many happy Christmases to come.

THE END